GIRLS FLY!

by Lynn M. Homan and
Thomas Reilly

illustrated by
Rosalie M. Shepherd

PELICAN PUBLISHING COMPANY
Gretna 2003

For my nephew Patrick, the aviator in the family—L. M. H.
For my heroes, Charlene Reilly and Tony Jannus—T. R.

Library of Congress Cataloging-in-Publication Data

Homan, Lynn M.
    Girls fly! / by Lynn M. Homan and Thomas Reilly ; illustrated by Rosalie M. Shepherd.
    p. cm.
Summary: When Charlene's brothers tell her that she cannot be a pilot because she is a girl, she gives them a lesson in the rich history of women in flight.
    ISBN 1-58980-154-7 (hardcover : alk. paper)
    [1. Sex role—Fiction. 2. Air pilots—Fiction. 3. Self-actualization—Fiction. 4. Flight—History—Fiction.] I. Reilly, Thomas. II. Shepherd, Rosalie M., ill. III. Title.
    PZ7.H74373 Gi 2003
    [E]—dc21
                          2003008471

Printed in Korea
Published by Pelican Publishing Company, Inc.
1000 Burmaster Street, Gretna, Louisiana 70053

GIRLS FLY!

"Charlene, what do you want to be when you grow up?"
"I'm going to be a pilot. I'm going to fly an airplane!"
Charlene told her brothers.

"Charlene, girls can't fly airplanes," Tommy argued.
"That's right. Girls aren't big enough or strong enough to handle giant airplanes like that one," added Patrick.

"You don't know what you're talking about," responded Charlene. "Women have been flying airplanes almost as long as men have. Besides, I can do anything that either of you can and that includes being a pilot. Girls fly!"

"No way, Charlene," teased Patrick.

"You guys just don't have a clue," continued Charlene. "Just a few years after Orville and Wilbur Wright made the first-ever airplane flight, Baroness Raymonde de la Roche earned her pilot's license."

"That's not all. Years before the Wright brothers' first flight, Leila Marie Cody flew in a kite."

"You mean she flew a kite," Tommy corrected.

"No, silly. She flew *in* a kite," answered Charlene.

"In the early days of flying, women performed at airshows all over the country just like the men did," Charlene told her brothers. "They did tricks and won airplane races."

"Hmmm," said Patrick.

"Did you know that a woman was the first African-American licensed to fly?"

Patrick and Tommy shook their heads.

"Bessie Coleman earned her license in 1921. She had to go to France to learn to fly because no one in the United States would teach her," said Charlene.

"Women pilots can do everything men can. They've flown blimps, gliders, helicopters, balloons, just everything. You've both heard of Amelia Earhart?"

"Yeah. She flew a long time ago, didn't she?" asked Tommy.

"Right," said Charlene. "Back in 1932, Amelia Earhart was the first woman to fly across the Atlantic Ocean by herself. She helped to start the 'Ninety-Nines,' an organization for women pilots, and was even their first president. She's still one of the world's best-known woman pilots."

"Amelia Earhart didn't complete her around-the-world flight, but other women have," continued Charlene.

"Name one," challenged Patrick.

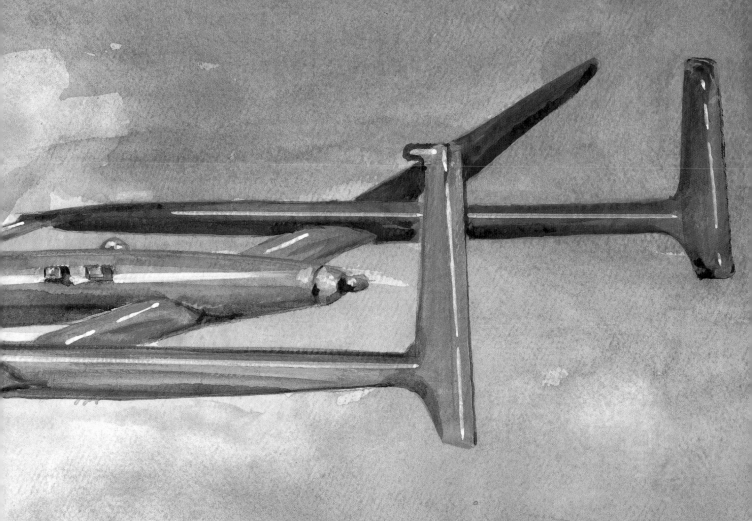

"Jeana Yeager," answered Charlene. "In 1986, she and Dick Rutan made an around-the-world nonstop flight. They flew 216 hours without landing and set a record."

"Awesome," said Patrick.

"You've both heard of Charles Lindbergh, haven't you?" asked Charlene.

"You betcha," said Patrick.

"Sure," agreed Tommy. "He was the first person to fly across the Atlantic Ocean all by himself."

"But did you know that his wife, Anne Morrow Lindbergh, was also a pilot?"
Both boys shook their heads.
"She flew all over the world with him. Besides that, she was the first American woman to earn a glider pilot's license."

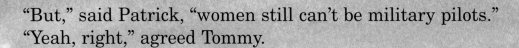

"But," said Patrick, "women still can't be military pilots."

"Yeah, right," agreed Tommy.

"For your information, smarty, women flew as WASPs and ferry pilots during World War II," said Charlene.

"The members of the Women Airforce Service Pilots program flew every kind of airplane that the military used. The women ferry pilots even delivered planes across the Atlantic Ocean to the war in Europe!"

"Wow," said Tommy.

"Well, that was way back then," argued Patrick.

"Yeah," agreed Tommy. "Women don't fly in the military today."

"You're both so wrong," countered Charlene. "Women began flying in the U.S. Navy in 1973 and with the Air Force three years later."

"And today, women fly all kinds of airplanes in every
branch of the military," Charlene continued.
"But not in combat," argued Patrick.
"Oh, yes!" said Charlene. "Even in combat!"

"Charlene, you talked about women pilots performing tricks,"
said Tommy. "I bet they were easy stunts."

"No way, Tommy. Pilots like Betty Skelton and Patty Wagstaff
could do every trick that the male pilots could do!"

"Like what?" Tommy asked.

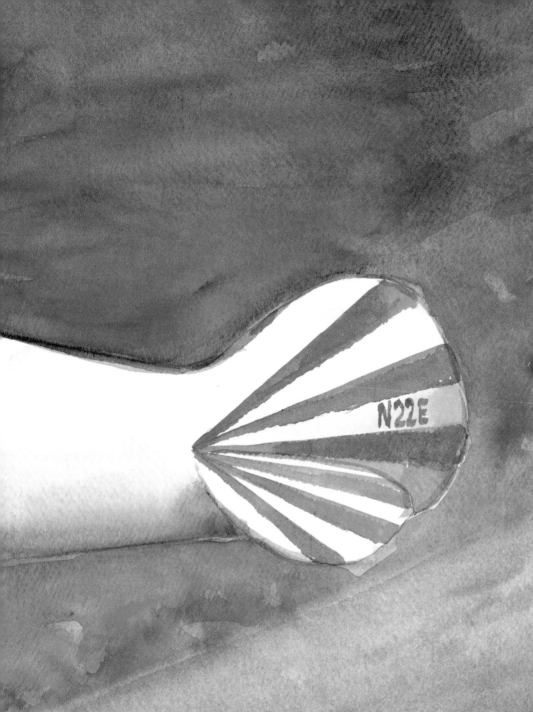

"They could do loops, rolls, and lots of aerobatic tricks," answered Charlene. "Betty Skelton became really famous flying her airplane named *Little Stinker.*"

"I didn't know that," Tommy said.

"Me neither," Patrick admitted.

"Remember when Dad took us to watch hot-air balloons?" asked Charlene.

"Definitely," said Patrick.

"Way back in 1880, Mary Myers was the first American woman to pilot a balloon. Her nickname was 'Carlotta, the Lady Aeronaut' and everybody knew about her."

"You know, 'aeronaut' sounds a lot like 'astronaut.' I know you two have seen real women astronauts on TV. Sally Ride was the first American female astronaut to fly on a space mission, way back in 1983."

"The first *American* woman?" asked Patrick.

"Yes," said Charlene. "A Russian named Valentina Tereshkova was the first woman in the world to do it."

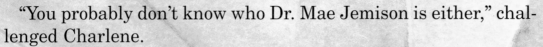

"You probably don't know who Dr. Mae Jemison is either," challenged Charlene.

Again, both boys shook their heads.

"She was the first African-American woman astronaut. She flew in space in 1992."

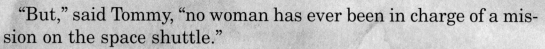

"But," said Tommy, "no woman has ever been in charge of a mission on the space shuttle."

"Wrong," replied Charlene. "Obviously you've never heard of Eileen Collins. She commanded the space shuttle in 1999."

"Let me tell you something else. Dr. Shannon Lucid has flown on so many missions that she's spent more time in space than any other American, man or woman."

"I'll bet women haven't been flying for airlines very long, though," challenged Patrick.

"Sure they have. Way back in 1934, Central Airlines hired Helen Richey as a pilot. She flew a Ford trimotor airplane that carried twenty-six passengers."

"There are lots of women airline pilots now,"
Charlene told her brothers.

"I can be just like all of these women.
Girls can be anything they want to be."